• Mr Wi[illegible] •

Hilary Sharpe •

Illustrated by
Rowan Barnes Murphy

Chapter 1
An Unusual Animal

Mr Willoughby dropped his bag of buns. He always brought buns for the animals when he came to the zoo, and somehow he nearly always dropped some. The bag landed upside down on the grass, scattering buns in all directions.

Mr Willoughby sighed, and tried to put his foot on the bag, but the wind decided to join in the fun and blew it out of reach. Mr Willoughby's droopy grey moustache drooped even further. The zoo keepers didn't like people who dropped litter. He looked around guiltily, in case someone might have seen him.

Someone had. Two someones. Not keepers, but Mr Willoughby's neighbours at home.

Pauline lived next door to him on one side, and Arthur, who was in the same class at school as Pauline, lived on the other. Sometimes they shouted to each other across Mr Willoughby's garden.

Pauline shouted now. "Hi, Mr Willoughby!"

Arthur picked up one of the buns and bowled it overarm to him. Much to his own surprise, Mr Willoughby caught it. Pauline ran after the bag and together they collected all the buns.

"I'm afraid they're a bit muddy," Pauline said. "I hope they weren't for your tea?"

"They're for the elephants, stupid," said Arthur. "Aren't they, Mr Willoughby?"

"Er – yes. Mostly. The lions don't seem to like buns very much."

Arthur and Pauline laughed politely and Mr Willoughby looked surprised. He hadn't realized he'd made a joke.

"Our class at school is doing a project about animals this term," Arthur said, "so we thought we'd come and look at zoo animals."

"Do you have a favourite animal, Mr Willoughby?" Pauline asked as they walked together towards the elephants. Mr Willoughby's moustache perked up a bit and the tip of his nose went pink.

"Well – I like the elephants of course – and the penguins. But really, it's the kangaroos and wallabies that I – " He coughed, and his nose went a deeper shade of pink.

Fancy a funny old person like Mr W liking big, bouncing kangaroos, Arthur thought! You'd expect him to prefer timid things like mice or koalas.

"We've talked to some of the keepers here, and people we know, about their favourite animals," said Pauline, "but it's dead boring. We want something unusual."

"Why don't you ask the animals what they think about people, then?" Mr Willoughby asked unexpectedly.

Pauline and Arthur stared at him.

"Ask the animals? How do you do that?"

"Here, Mr Elephant, do you like us?" Arthur offered one of Mr Willoughby's buns to the largest elephant, who took it politely.

"He likes your buns, anyway," Arthur laughed.

"He's enjoying himself," said Mr Willoughby. "Look at his eyes." The elephant's eyes certainly seemed to be twinkling as he waved his trunk about in search of more buns.

"Some animals like to be talked to," Mr Willoughby went on, "others aren't interested. You have to watch their faces. Of course, it doesn't have to be just zoo animals."

"Well, that's different, anyway," Pauline said. "Come on, Art, let's go and interview the camels!"

They ran ahead, laughing. Mr Willoughby followed more slowly. The camels stared into space or looked haughtily down their noses at them, so they went to talk to the llamas. The llamas liked having their necks tickled and nodded their heads up and down. The snakes, however, ignored the children completely.

"They're probably very hurt when people say, 'Ugh!' and shudder," said Mr Willoughby.

When they reached the kangaroo enclosure Mr Willoughby made a funny little chirrupy noise and several of the animals looked up. Presently one of them hopped over and put its nose through the fence. Mr Willoughby stroked it.

"This one's a wallaby," he said. "They are smaller than kangaroos. She's a young one, her name's Willa."

"Willa Wallaby!" Arthur grinned. Willa fluttered her eyelashes at Mr Willoughby and turned her large bright eyes on the children. She twitched her ears at them and then bounded away and began to browse on the grass.

"She doesn't think much of us," Pauline laughed. "Let's go and see what the monkeys think."

Mr Willoughby walked home slowly. It was late tea-time and there were not many people about, but once or twice he felt as though someone was following him. He looked round, but he couldn't see anyone. Some rude boys trying to tease him, he thought.

He went into the kitchen and put the kettle on for his tea. He was just going

to cut the bread for a cheese and lettuce sandwich when he dropped the bread knife with a clatter. There was somebody looking in at the kitchen window! Those rude boys must have followed him home!

“Go away, boy,” he called hoarsely. The face at the window didn’t move, but it put out its tongue and licked the glass. Mr Willoughby stared. It didn’t look like a boy’s face. It had a long nose, big upright ears and fur!

"Willa!" Mr Willoughby shouted. He flung open the back door and Willa hopped into the kitchen. She wuffled her nose at him. Mr Willoughby swallowed nervously. He looked outside the kitchen door, but there was nobody there.

"How did you get here, Willa?" he cried. "Did somebody bring you?" Willa didn't say a word, but she noticed the lettuce waiting to be put into Mr Willoughby's sandwich. She reached out a paw, sniffed at the lettuce, and began to nibble it.

"Oh dear, oh dear, whatever am I going to do with you?" wailed Mr Willoughby.

"Perhaps you're hungry?" he said, when Willa had finished the lettuce. He looked in his larder and found a cabbage. Willa nibbled that too. Then she lay down on the kitchen floor, sighed contentedly, and dozed.

Mr Willoughby made his tea-time sandwich – just cheese, since Willa had eaten his lettuce – and decided he must telephone the zoo. He picked up the receiver and put it down again. The zoo might think he had stolen her. The best thing would be to take her back after dark and hope no one would see them.

He sat down to wait. There wasn't much room to move about his little kitchen with Willa sprawled on the floor. At last he said, "Willa dear, you'll have to go home, I can't keep you here."

Willa looked up at him for a long, long moment. Then, to his horror, he saw two big fat tears running down her cheeks.

He wrung his hands. "Please don't cry, Willa." Poor Mr Willoughby was nearly crying himself. "I didn't know wallabies could cry like that."

With a sweep of her long black eyelashes Willa closed her eyes and squeezed out two more big tears. Mr Willoughby tried to pace up and down his kitchen, stepping carefully on bits of floor not occupied by Willa, and nearly falling over her large feet.

"Oh dear, oh dear." Mr Willoughby moved Willa's tail from his coal scuttle and sighed again.

Suddenly he had an idea. There was a shed in the garden where he kept his gardening tools. He could put Willa in there for tonight. And tomorrow – well, tomorrow he would see.

Willa followed him happily into the shed. He had found an old dog bowl which he filled with water in case she got thirsty in the night. He turned it round so that Willa wouldn't see the word "dog" written on it. He patted her nose goodnight, closed the door firmly and went back to the house.

It was a nice bright morning when Mr Willoughby woke up. He felt quite bright and cheery himself. Then he remembered Willa. Perhaps the zoo wouldn't notice that she had gone. Perhaps he could keep her in the shed. Wouldn't the neighbours be surprised when he took her for walks! He would have to get in lots of greenstuff to feed her on. He had better get up, Willa would be wanting her breakfast.

When he went downstairs he was actually humming a little tune. Then he opened his back door – and gasped.

Most of his garden seemed to have disappeared. The grass in his little back garden had been nibbled down to the roots, there was hardly a leaf to be seen on his neat little bushes, and the hedge looked like a row of spiky sticks!

The shed door was open, and Willa, with a suspiciously fat-looking tummy, was lying on the garden path and dozing in the early morning sunshine.

Chapter 2
Wilful Wallaby

"Tell you what," said Arthur, as he and Pauline dawdled home from school next day, "Mr W said to find out what animals think, and not just zoo animals, so why don't we interview all the kids in our class who've got animals, and ask, 'What does your pet think of you?' That's a lot more unusual than asking what they think of their pets!"

"Great! 'My dog whines all day when I'm at school...' "

" 'My sister's cat scratches her...' "

" 'My parrot spits nutshells at me...' "

"Then there's goldfish... rabbits... mice..."

Pauline made gobbling noises and Arthur squeaked and screwed up his nose, to the disgust of a lady coming in the opposite direction.

"Such manners," she muttered, as they hastily turned into the little lane which ran behind their gardens.

"We could ask Willa what she thinks about Mr Willoughby next time we go to the zoo," Arthur grinned, vaulting his back gate. "See you."

Pauline had to walk past Mr Willoughby's garden to get to her own. Suddenly, she stopped and stared.

"Art!" she shouted, "Come and look at this!"

"What's up?"

"Looks like locusts have been at Mr Willoughby's garden!"

"Great jumping cracker beans!" Arthur exclaimed when he saw the damage, "I hope they haven't eaten Mr Willoughby as well."

"Come on," Pauline cried. They opened Mr Willoughby's gate and charged up the path. Mr Willoughby heard them coming and rushed out of the house, thinking Willa had escaped again. They almost met head-on and had to do a little dance round each other to avoid falling over.

"Whatever happened?" gasped Pauline.

"Shh," said Mr Willoughby, "don't wake her up."

"Who?"

"Willa. You'd better come inside and I'll tell you."

They sat in Mr Willoughby's kitchen and he told them all about Willa following him home, and how he had put her in the shed.

"She must have been hungry, poor little creature," he explained. "She broke open the shed door and ate all the grass and plants. I suppose it's not a very big garden really, compared to her paddock at the zoo."

"Where is she now?" asked Arthur.

"Asleep in the shed. I mended the door, but when she wakes up she'll be hungry again. I suppose that now I'll have to take her straight back to the zoo."

He gave such a deep, sad sigh that Pauline felt quite sorry for him. She patted his shoulder comfortingly.

"Perhaps you could keep her for just one more day?" she suggested.

Arthur had a sudden idea. "Didn't you once have a dog, Mr Willoughby?"

"Yes. Dear old Rover. We were together for fourteen years."

"Do you still have his collar and lead?"

"Why yes! Would you like to see them?" Mr Willoughby got up and rummaged about in the dresser drawer.

"They're somewhere about – I kept his water bowl too, Willa has it in the shed – ah, here they are."

He brought out a thick leather collar, lovingly polished, and a strong lead.

"Great," said Arthur, "just what we need. We'd better go home for tea now, you know what parents are, but when it's dark we'll come round and help you take Willa for a walk in the park. There's loads of grass and stuff there for her to eat."

It was dusk when they set out. Luckily it wasn't far to the park. They met one old gentleman walking his dog. The dog set up a furious barking until Willa bounded towards him, then he turned tail and ran off, howling and dragging his astonished owner behind him. At the corner of the street the dog-owner spotted a policeman.

"Officer," he puffed, "I've just seen a kangaroo hopping down the street!"

"Really, sir?" The policeman was on his way home after a long day on duty.

"It was wearing a collar and lead. I tell you – "

"Right you are, sir. I'll take care of it. I should get along home now, if I were you."

Kangaroos in collars, the policeman thought wearily, whatever next? As if he hadn't enough to do trying to solve the Case of the Stolen Pizzas. Nearly every take-away pizza place in town had had some pizzas stolen recently. Still, he supposed he should take a look. He looked, but the road was deserted.

The park was nearly empty as they made for a lonely part where the grass hadn't been cut recently. Willa settled down to browse.

"We had better keep hold of her lead," said Mr Willoughby, "just in case."

As Willa nibbled daintily, Mr Willoughby asked how their work on animals was getting on, and Pauline, who was holding the lead, was just about to tell him, when she was suddenly jerked into the air. For a second she thought she was flying, until she landed with a bump in some thick grass. Willa had finished all the grass round her and had bounded to another patch that had taken her eye, whisking Pauline behind her.

"Whoooosh! Huff!" Pauline gasped.

"Hang on to her, bird-brain!" Arthur yelled, as Pauline dropped the lead to brush the grass off herself. Willa looked up, and before Pauline could

grab the lead again she had bounded further into the grass and bushes. Arthur rushed after her with another yell, while Mr Willoughby murmured, “Don’t shout, children, you’ll scare her off.”

It was soon evident that no human could keep up with a wallaby in full flight. The last they saw of her she was leaping across the grass and disappearing again among the trees.

Chapter 3
Picnic in the Park

"You silly ass," Arthur said, "fancy letting go of her lead."

"Bet you'd have let go if you'd suddenly been bounced into the air like that," Pauline said crossly. "Ass yourself."

"I do hope she didn't hurt you, my dear," Mr Willoughby said anxiously.

"Oh, she'll survive – but look, Willa's getting away."

"She won't go far," said Mr Willoughby. "She'll have stopped to browse again."

They set off in the direction Willa had taken, but she was nowhere to be seen. It was quite dark now as well, which didn't help. In the gloom they zigzagged across the park, calling "Willa!" softly from time to time. Sometimes they heard the faint thud of large feet and once they caught a glimpse of her speeding across some open ground before disappearing once more into the trees. Presently, the moon came out to help them.

The railings at the far side of the park were in sight when Mr Willoughby said at last, "It's no use, we shall have to leave her. Your parents will be wondering where you are."

They went back across the park and soon reached the little stream that ran through one corner of it. It was muddy on the edge. Very muddy. There were large pawprints in the mud and very little else. Instead of the usual water plants beside the stream there were only a few discarded flower heads.

Pauline and Arthur stared at each other, aghast. "Gosh!" they said together.

"Oh dear," said Mr Willoughby.

They tried to follow the direction of the paw marks, which wasn't easy. Willa didn't hop in a straight line, she went in every which direction, and the marks crossed and recrossed each other until the sleuths didn't know whether they were following or leading.

Suddenly, Mr Willoughby gave a shout. Ahead of them were the bushes and trees of the wild garden, left especially for the bees and butterflies and wild birds. The moon was well up now, and shone helpfully on... Willa, munching her way through the long grass, nettles and brambles.

Completely forgetting to approach her quietly, they all raced towards her, shouting, "Willa, WILLA!" Suddenly Willa looked up, startled, and bounded away into the distance.

"Great galloping jellyfish," Arthur exclaimed, "now what do we do?"

"Go home," said Pauline, "I've had enough."

"That was most foolish of me," Mr Willoughby scolded himself, "I should have coaxed her quietly."

They walked slowly past the ruined wild garden and tried not to look at the bare patches where the nettles had been, and the bushes with no leaves.

"How can a small wallaby have such a huge appetite?" wondered Pauline.

"I don't know, but somebody's going to get into trouble for all this damage," said Arthur gloomily.

Mr Willoughby groaned.

Dejectedly, they set off again. Then Pauline noticed the odd-shaped hedge by the notice saying "Exotic Plants."

"Oh NO!" she gasped.

"Surely not?" murmured Mr Willoughby. "Wallabies like plain food."

"This one's got a taste for tropical delicacies," Arthur said, leading the way into the Exotic Plant garden. Fortunately, a lot of the plants were safely inside greenhouses, but a small grove of lemon and orange trees seemed to be suspicously short of leaves, and so did the magnolia bushes. Willa had sampled the azaleas and tried a few lotus plants beside the ornamental lake, but of the wallaby herself there was no sign.

The off-duty policeman had just been called back on duty. There had been yet another daring raid on a take-away pizza parlour, and he was not happy. Suddenly, he saw a dark outline coming towards him. An unlighted vehicle, approaching very fast. Could this be a van full of stolen pizzas?

The policeman held up his hand, thinking of the glory of capture. "STOP, in the name of the law!" he roared. But the vehicle didn't. It actually *hopped* past him, and in the light of a street lamp the policeman could have sworn it was a kangaroo.

He took off his helmet and mopped his forehead. Either he'd been overdoing things, or he needed glasses.

Chapter 4
Invasion!

Much to their relief, Mr Willoughby, Pauline and Arthur got back to find Willa comfortably settled in her shed, and snoring happily. Mr Willoughby put a padlock on the door this time.

After school next day, Arthur had a music lesson and Pauline went to karate club, so it was evening before they could go and see Mr Willoughby again. Mr Willoughby's droopy moustache was even limper than usual, and he had some extra wrinkles on his forehead, Pauline noticed. Arthur thought he looked like a sad walrus.

"What did the zoo people say?" Arthur asked.

"I – er, I haven't phoned them yet. It seemed a shame to disturb her, you know. She's slept all day."

"I can believe it," Arthur said with feeling.

"Don't you think you'd better phone them before she wakes up and gets hungry again?" Pauline suggested.

"Yes, I'm afraid you're right," sighed Mr Willoughby. "Would you like to go and say goodbye to her first?"

Willa didn't move when they opened the shed door.

"Bye, Willa," Pauline said, dropping a kiss on the top of Willa's sleeping head.

"See you in the zoo," said Arthur.

With a heart-rending sigh, Mr Willoughby closed, padlocked and bolted the shed door. (He had put new bolts on the outside of the door, top and bottom, and on the window.)

"It's rather late," he said hesitantly, "I think perhaps if I phone tomorrow morning...? She's safe enough now."

"Here we go again," Arthur muttered, but Pauline thought how sad the poor little man looked. "Never mind," she comforted him, "you'll be able to visit her again at the zoo."

"If I'm allowed to," said Mr Willoughby.

As they parted at Mr Willoughby's back gate, Arthur said enthusiastically, "I'm going to bring my camera over tomorrow – you can take a photo of me asking Willa what she thinks of Mr Willoughby!"

"Oh, go and eat worms," Pauline snapped.

Arthur was awakened early next morning, which happened to be a Saturday, by an agitated phone call from Pauline.

"I can see Mr Willoughby's shed from my bedroom window," she cried, "and the door's open."

"It'll be the zoo men collecting Willa," Arthur said sleepily.

"They wouldn't take the door off its hinges, it's sort of hanging sideways!"

Both children dressed at top speed and rushed off without waiting for breakfast, much to their parents' surprise. They found Mr Willoughby staring in amazement at the broken hinges on his shed door.

"Strong, isn't she?" said Arthur.

"She was here an hour ago," Mr Willoughby cried anxiously, "I came out early to see that she was all right."

"She probably hasn't gone far then," said Pauline.

They rushed off and were half way down the road before they realized they didn't know which way to go.

"She knows the park," Pauline said, "she could have gone there again."

When they reached the park they found a gang of gardeners still repairing the damage Willa had done before. Somehow, it didn't seem a good

time to ask if they'd seen a wallaby anywhere.

They trailed slowly back home, looking about them, and presently saw a group of people all talking at once and staring into someone's front garden.

"Vandals!" A fat man was bouncing up and down angrily and shaking his fists. "I'll have the law on them!"

"Never seen such a mess."

"Ever such a pretty border he had."

"Those apple trees'll be no good for a year or two, I shouldn't wonder."

"More like a ploughed field than a lawn!"

The group of people shook their heads and tut-tutted. Mr Willoughby groaned and tiptoed past them.

"We'd better find her quickly," Arthur said anxiously.

It wasn't hard to follow her trail. Further down the road they saw another puzzled group, this time outside a garden centre.

"Clearly the damage has been caused by some unnatural visitation," an important-looking man was saying.

"What, like spacemen?"

"No, no, my dear madam – ha, ha, we aren't in the realms of science fiction!"

"Well, it's something big, or lots of them," said another man, pushing his cap back and scratching his bald head.

"Cor! Come and look at this – a giant footprint!" yelled a small boy with sharp eyes. The crowd surged forward. There, in a muddy patch between trays of chewed lettuce plants, was a clear impression of Willa's large feet.

"It's a lion, an escaped lion! Come away, Terry!" a woman screamed, dragging her protesting son away from the paw marks.

"Calm yourself, madam," said the important-looking man, "lions are carnivores, they don't eat lettuce."

"Maybe he fancied a salad starter," muttered the bald man. The crowd moved rapidly away.

Arthur also had sharp eyes. "Look," he whispered, "muddy pawprints on the pavement. Come on."

They followed the pawprints down a side street. Ahead of them was a greengrocer's shop, and the enraged shopkeeper was staring at a tray of apples scattered on the pavement, an overturned box of sprouts, and several cabbages which were lying in the gutter.

"You can't trust anyone these days," he snapped to Mr Willoughby. "I'd only just set up my trestle table outside the shop window. Nice display of red apples and green veggies on it, catches the eye, y'see, and folk come inside and see what else you've got. Only left it for a few minutes to answer the phone. Didn't see anyone about, I suppose?" he asked hopefully.

"I did, Mister!" A small, freckle-faced girl was looking out of the window of the house opposite. "It wasn't anybody. Not a person. It was an animal that knocked over the boxes and took the apples!"

The shopkeeper went red in the face with fury and shook his fist in the direction of the small girl. "Don't you be telling me fibs, Rosie Anderson. Filled his shopping trolley with my best fruit I suppose? Animal indeed!"

"It's true, Mister!" Another freckled face appeared beside the first one. "I saw it too. It was a dinosaur. We've done dinosaurs at school. It had a long neck and a great big tail and it hopped..." The shopkeeper let out a roar of fury and the two freckled faces disappeared from the window.

"A dinosaur that hopped! Maybe it had wings too!" roared the shopkeeper. "I reckon I'd better come over and have a word with your mum, young Rosie."

"Er – can we help you tidy up?" Mr Willoughby asked quickly, picking up two cabbages from the gutter and putting them on the trestle table.

"Well, much obliged, I'm sure." The greengrocer glared in the direction of the empty window and turned back to rescue his vegetables. There didn't seem to be much missing, at any rate, Mr Willoughby thought as they picked up the last apple and went on their way again.

But it wasn't long before they were in the thick of another commotion. "The whole town must be out this morning," Pauline gasped. In the middle of yet another crowd of people a policeman was taking notes. A man on the edge of the crowd turned as Mr Willoughby and the children came running up.

"That's the latest, that is," he grinned, "we've been invaded by folk dressed as kangaroos, if this lot are to be believed. Hopping about all over town. I wonder what they'll think of next?" He walked away, chuckling.

"We'd better go home and telephone the zoo," Mr Willoughby said. "There's no point in looking any further, she could be anywhere."

"Oh, I do hope nobody hurts her," Pauline puffed.

"They'll have to catch her first," Arthur said grimly.

Ahead of them, someone was shouting. They raced round a corner to see two women pointing up the road. "A kangaroo! I tell you it was a kangaroo!" one of them screamed.

"She's going home," Arthur yelled. "COME ON!"

They rushed into the garden, to find Willa sitting calmly outside the shed. When she saw Mr Willoughby she put her paw inside her pouch, drew out a rosy apple, and offered it to him.

Chapter 5
Thief-Catcher

Mr Willoughby led Willa into the kitchen, where she sat on the hearthrug and emptied her pouch.

"She thinks she's brought you a present," Pauline gulped, hoping she wasn't going to disgrace herself by bursting into tears. Mr Willoughby stared mournfully at Willa, his thin, grey moustache drooping even more than usual. Arthur cleared his throat and began to count, rather huskily, "Five red apples, six – no, seven sprouts and a small cabbage."

There was silence for a moment, then Mr Willoughby sighed, "I must phone the zoo right away."

"I hope they won't be too angry," Pauline whispered.

"They're sending a van for her," Mr Willoughby said as he put the phone down. "They sounded most relieved to hear that she was safe." He collected up the fruit and vegetables. Pauline sat on the floor with her arms round Willa, who was dozing happily.

There was another silence, until Arthur suddenly announced, "We haven't had any breakfast!"

Pauline glared at him, but Mr Willoughby said, "I'll make some toast while we're waiting."

He bustled about with bread and teacups, and put on the kettle. Then there was more silence, so he turned on the radio. A cheerful voice from the local radio station informed them that today would be bright and sunny. The voice went on to say, "The take-away pizza thieves struck again last night when the Pisa Pizza Parlour on Main Street was raided. The pizza thieves got away with several dozen fresh pizzas. The police are baffled and the Pizza Parlour owners are offering a reward for any information leading to the capture of the theives..."

The radio droned on as Mr Willoughby put plates of buttered toast on the table. Silently, he poured the tea, and silently Pauline and Arthur sat at the table.

It was a relief to all of them when the zoo van arrived. Willa was quite pleased to see her keeper again. He accepted a cup of tea from Mr Willoughby, whom he recognised as a regular visitor to the zoo.

"I've been off work with the flu, you see, so Willa wasn't missed till I got back yesterday. Then we had a right old search, I can tell you! 'Course, we didn't want to make it public, didn't want people to panic, y'know. Didn't want to risk her getting hurt either. Mind, I can see you've taken good care of her." He smiled at all three of them, gulped down his tea and stood up.

"Come on Willa, my girl. Holiday over now, time to go home."

He took one of Willa's paws and led her outside to the waiting van. Willa hopped inside and the keeper got in beside her. Sadly, they waved her off.

"Now," said Mr Willoughby briskly, "we'll go back to the greengrocer and pay for this fruit."

They hadn't gone far when they came upon the zoo van standing in a little side street between a children's playground and a take-away called the Vegetarian Pizza House. The driver was looking at the van in disgust.

"Just my luck," he said to Mr Willoughby, "I've got a flat tyre. Had to turn in here to change the wheel." He banged on the back door of the van. "Open up, Charlie," he shouted to the keeper.

Charlie opened the door, the driver reached inside the van for his tools – and then everything seemed to happen at once!

Willa poked her head out and saw Mr Willoughby. Before Charlie could stop her she had leapt out of the van, hopped over to him and licked his face. Mr Willoughby tripped over her big feet, lost his balance and sat down on the pavement, which startled Willa into jumping over the railings of the children's playground.

"STOP her!" bawled her keeper. At that moment the doors of the Vegetarian Pizza House flew open and two masked men, each carrying a large pile of vegetarian pizzas, shot out and rushed towards a mini parked behind the zoo van.

Then, suddenly, both men stopped dead in their tracks and stared with their mouths open. Willa had hopped on to one of the children's swings and was swinging up and down, a blissful smile on her face. The pizza thieves couldn't believe their eyes!

The next moment a police car, in search of Willa, raced along the street and screeched to a stop. Two policemen leapt out and advanced upon Willa. All of a sudden they noticed the thieves, still standing there with their mouths open and their arms full of pizzas. With quiet efficiency they arrested the thieves, while Mr Willoughby, Pauline, Arthur and the zoo men tried to catch Willa!

But Willa was enjoying herself. She had just hopped from the swing to a roundabout when Arthur had a brainwave. Quickly he grabbed a pizza that the thieves had dropped, and held it out to Willa. An appetizing smell of freshly-cooked vegetables and herbs rose from it. Willa took it daintily in her paw, sniffed at it, and settled down to enjoy it.

Chapter 6
"Willa Thinks You're Ace!"

"So you're saying that Willa the Wallaby should really have the reward for the capture of the pizza thieves?" asked Mike, the local radio station reporter.

"Definitely," said Arthur. "If she hadn't been on that swing when the thieves came out of the pizza place, they'd have got to their getaway car before anyone could have stopped them!"

Mike had called at Mr Willoughby's house later that day to interview the three of them. Pauline and Arthur were thoroughly enjoying it, but poor Mr Willoughby wasn't. His nose was bright pink and so were the tips of his ears.

"And what do you think Willa should do with the reward?" asked Mike.

"Perhaps she could give it to the park people for some new plants?" Pauline suggested.

Mr Willoughby's grey moustache drooped with embarrassment. "I'm afraid it wouldn't be nearly enough," he murmured.

"You could always give them the reward the zoo offered you for catching Willa," Arthur said.

"I wouldn't dream of accepting a reward," Mr Willoughby said indignantly. "I should feel I'd betrayed her trust."

Mike looked thoughtfully at Mr Willoughby. "Tell us about Willa," he invited.

Hesitantly, with the help of Arthur and Pauline, he told Mike how Willa had come to his house, and all the things that had happened before she had finally got back to the zoo.

"We all went in the van with her," Pauline said, "and when the keeper put her back in her enclosure he found she'd got another pizza in her pouch!"

"You'll have to take her one as a treat whenever you go and visit her," Arthur laughed.

“At any rate, we don’t have to interview Willa to find out what she thinks about you, Mr Willoughby,” Pauline said. “She thinks you’re ace!”

Mr Willoughby’s nose and ears turned a deeper pink as Arthur groaned, “Great jumping carrot flies, I’d forgotten about the animal interviews!”

Mike, who had been about to put away his notebook, opened it again. “Animal interviews?” he asked.

So they told him about their topic on animals, and how Mr Willoughby had suggested they find out what animals thought about people.

“That would certainly be something different,” Mike said, “but why don’t you just write Willa’s story?”

Pauline looked doubtful. "Would people believe it was real and not made up? We know it's true of course, but would they believe us at school?"

"I should think they'd wonder how anyone could be so silly as to let a little wallaby do so much damage," Mr Willoughby said unhappily.

"You're not to blame yourself," Pauline scolded, "it's not your fault she's got such a huge appetite."

"Well," said Mike, "our listeners will be very interested to hear Willa's story, so let's see what they have to say about it, shall we?"

The listeners, many of whom were most relieved to hear that they were not in any danger from a dinosaur or an invasion of spacemen, took Mr

Willoughby and his wallaby to their hearts. The local newspaper took up the story with the rather inaccurate headline, "Brave Willa Wallaby foils daring pizza thieves" and started a fund to pay for the damage she had done.

Before long, so many readers and listeners had subscribed to it that there was enough money to replace the plants in the park and the garden centre, with enough left over for the man whose front garden Willa had chewed up. Mr Willoughby refused to take any money to replace his lawn, but he remembered to go and see the greengrocer and pay him for the apples and greens Willa had brought home in her pouch.

Pauline and Arthur did write about Willa for their animal study, but unfortunately it got mixed up at school. It was entered for the Fantasy Story competition instead – and won first prize!

"Fantastic!" cried Arthur, but Pauline was disgusted.

She went with Mr Willoughby to see Willa, and they took her some rosy red apples and a pizza from the Vegetarian Pizza House.